Grandpa's Teeth

ROD CLEMENT

Grandpa's

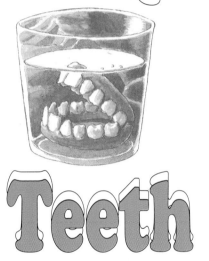

Teeth

HARPERCOLLINS*PUBLISHERS*

For Carla, Lucy, and Kitty

Grandpa's Teeth
Copyright © 1997 by Rod Clement
First published in 1997 by HarperCollinsPublishers Pty Limited,
25 Ryde Road, Pymble, Sydney, NSW 2073, Australia.
Printed in the U.S.A. All rights reserved.

Library of Congress Cataloging-in-Publication Data
Clement, Rod.
  Grandpa's teeth / Rod Clement.
    p.   cm.
  Summary: Soon after Grandpa's teeth disappear from a glass
of water near his bed, Officer Rate has the whole town under
investigation.
  ISBN 0-06-027671-1 — ISBN 0-06-443557-1 (pbk.)
  [1. Teeth—Fiction. 2. Grandfathers—Fiction. 3. Smile—Fiction.
4. Mystery and detective stories.] I. Title.
PZ7.C59114Gr 1998   97-14753
[E]—dc21   CIP
                                                          AC

Typography by Al Cetta
❖
First American Edition, 1998

Visit us on the World Wide Web!
http://www.harperchildrens.com

"**Help**, I've been robbed!" We heard Grandpa shouting. "It's*th* a dis*thasth*ter! Come quickly!"

He was still shouting as Mom, Agatha, and I ran up the stairs.

Grandpa's room was a mess, but to be honest, it was always a mess. He blamed Gump, his old dog, but Gump looked too old to me to make much of a mess.

"What was taken?" gasped Mom. "Your VCR? Your television? Not your gold-plated golfing trophy?"

"No," said Grandpa. "It's*th* much more s*th*erious. It's*th* my teeth—they've been s*th*tolen."

Grandpa normally kept his teeth in a glass of water by the bed. The glass was still there, but the teeth were missing.

"You haven't swallowed them by mistake, have you?" asked Mom.

"Of coursthe not!" replied Grandpa. "Thosthe teeth were sthpecial, handmade by the finestht Sthwissth craftsthmen!"

Agatha looked at Mom and whispered, "Why is Grandpa talking funny?"

"You sthee how stherious it isth?" moaned Grandpa. "I may never sthpeak the sthame again!"

"Are you sure you've looked everywhere?" asked
Mom. "Under the bed? Behind the cabinet? In
all the drawers?"

"Yes*th*," replied Grandpa with tears in his eyes.
"I've looked everywhere."

Mom called the police.

Officer Rate looked grave.

"We've done a thorough search of the room and house, but we've found nothing at all—no teeth, no clues. Everyone was at home at the time of the theft, so how the thief got in and out without being seen is a mystery."

They put up our WANTED poster with all the others.

We made copies and put them up all over town.

Officer Rate rounded up the usual suspects and took them in for questioning. All of them were asked to smile. Most of them had missing teeth as well, but just one or two—not the whole set.

They even brought in our unfriendly neighbor, Mrs. Carbuncle, because her own teeth didn't fit. But Grandpa didn't recognize her or the teeth in the police lineup.

"I've never *stheen* her *sthmile* before," he explained to Officer Rate.

After several days Officer Rate had to admit that no teeth had been found, no thief had been caught, and no new clues had been uncovered. Grandpa suspected everyone, especially anyone who didn't smile.

Soon the whole town was smiling at him, although he never smiled back—he had nothing to smile with.

Mom even got a call from one of those TV shows, *Unsolved Crimes*. They came to the house in a helicopter. We had to reenact the whole thing.

When Grandpa was interviewed, he asked the reporter, Pearl White, if he could borrow some of her teeth. "After all," he mumbled, "you have more than enough."

Dad called Switzerland to find out how much a new set of teeth would cost. He was so shocked when he found out that he dropped the phone.

"The only way we could ever afford it," he joked to Mom, "is to sell the house!"

Grandpa thought this was a great idea.

"Who needs*th* a hous*the* anyway?" he moaned. "It does*thn*'t help you chew your food!"

To cheer him up we all took Grandpa to the amusement park. It was a disaster. He took one look at the front entrance and burst into tears.

Everyone watched *Unsolved Crimes* but no one called Officer Rate, and the crime remained unsolved.

Some spare teeth were left in the mailbox, but none of them fit properly.

People began locking their doors at night, imagining a teeth thief loose on the streets. No one knew who would be next, so fear gripped the town.

The thief had to be caught—and soon!

It seemed that the only way to prove beyond a reasonable doubt that the teeth in your mouth were your own was to smile broadly at every person you met.

Anyone who didn't smile was immediately dragged off to the police station for more questions and a chat with Officer Rate.

So everyone began smiling at everyone else, all
the time, everywhere . . . even at funerals.

Because of Grandpa's teeth the whole town was beginning to suffer.

Tourists, seeing the endless sea of smiling faces, were too scared to get out of their cars.

After a while, they stopped coming altogether.
Dad's café, like the rest of the town, was losing
business.

The Mayor called an emergency meeting.

That night, for the first time that anyone could remember, the town hall was full. Speaker after speaker stood up to complain about the loss of customers and the constant strain of smiling all day, every day.

Pastor Butter summed up the situation. "While I've always considered this a happy town, there are limits! No one wants to smile without a reason, and there aren't many reasons to smile in this town at the moment. It's time, I believe, to put a stop to it!"

The crowd cheered.

"Mr. Pertwhistle had one of the finest sets of teeth in the country and he alone cannot afford to replace them. In fact, I alone could not afford to replace them either, but if every one of us put one dollar in the collection plate tonight, we would have enough money to buy two new sets of teeth!"

Most people put in a dollar. Others put in two.

At the presentation ceremony Grandpa opened
the package and revealed two sets of brand-new
teeth.

"Why are they different sizes?" asked the Mayor.

"Oh, only one of them is*th* for me," replied Grandpa, popping one of the sets into his mouth. "The other one is for Mrs. Carbuncle. Her teeth never fit properly, and she has such a pretty smile."

Grandpa was very happy with his new teeth. So was Mrs. Carbuncle. They smiled all the time.

In fact, they were so happy that Grandpa's old
dog, Gump, smiled too.

For the first time,
EVER!